This edition published by Parragon Books Ltd in 2014

Parragon Books Ltd
Chartist House
15–17 Trim Street
Bath BA1 1HA, UK
www.parragon.com

ISBN 978-1-4723-6305-3

Printed in China

Disney PRINCESS

Collection

Contents

Tangled
Ever After

Illustrated by Studio IBOIX

Spring had sprung and Flynn had a surprise for Rapunzel. They took a walk through the forest.

Flynn wanted to be alone with Rapunzel, but Maximus wanted to keep guard and Pascal went along to play.

Finally, evening came and Flynn took his chance to jump into a boat with Rapunzel. The lovely night reminded them of when they had first watched the floating lanterns together.

Flynn put his hand in his pocket – he was going to propose! But, oops, he did need Pascal and Max after all, because they had the ring!

"Will you marry me?" Flynn finally asked.
"Yes!" Rapunzel replied happily.

On their way home Rapunzel
wanted to tell everyone their news!

The thugs from The Snuggly Duckling were delighted.
It turned out they had always wanted a wedding to plan!
They each had their own ideas about the special day.

One of them helped Rapunzel to design a cake.

They baked and iced, but
nothing seemed quite right.
But, finally, they
created the wedding cake of
Rapunzel's dreams!

Next, Tor helped Rapunzel
choose the flowers.

Rapunzel's favourites were
the wild flowers picked
from a nearby field.

As for who would carry the rings –
the choice was easy! Maximus and Pascal
were very proud to accept.

When it was time to find a wedding dress
Rapunzel wanted to design her own. She drew lots
of pictures … but simply could not make up her mind!

The pub thugs tried to help, but their
dresses didn't seem right either.

Luckily, the Queen arrived.
"Darling," she said, "I want to
help you find the perfect dress."

And she did….

On the morning of the wedding, bells rang throughout the kingdom. Everyone was excited to see the King and Queen riding happily in the royal coach.

Max and Pascal were excited too – that is, until Max sneezed and the rings flew into the air!

As Max and Pascal chased after the rings, the King proudly offered his arm to Rapunzel to walk up the aisle.

Flynn was so happy when he saw
Rapunzel in her beautiful dress.
Luckily, nobody had any idea
what Max and Pascal were up to....

They were racing through the kingdom after the rings!
Max and Pascal were causing a lot of chaos.

Max ran straight through some
drying clothes as he chased one ring …

… and Pascal
chased the other ring
into the air.

They finally caught the runaway rings … but then they crashed right into the tar factory!

Max and Pascal quickly left the factory and raced to the wedding. They arrived just in time!

Even though their ring-bearers now looked a bit strange, Flynn and Rapunzel were glad they were there.

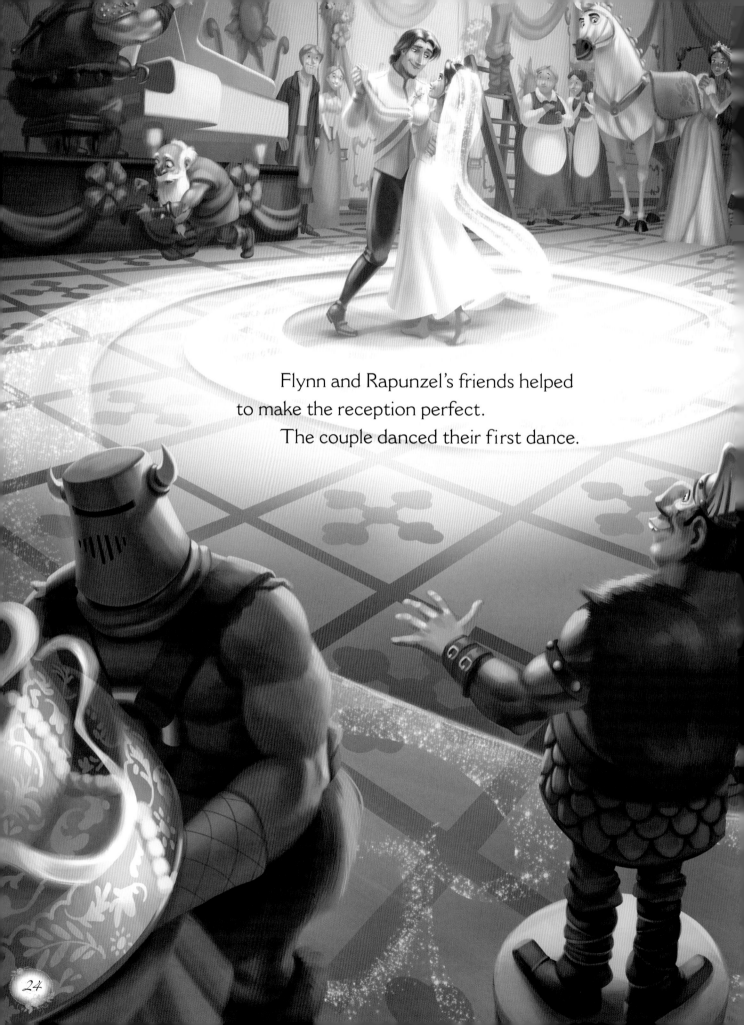

Flynn and Rapunzel's friends helped
to make the reception perfect.
The couple danced their first dance.

They cut the wedding cake
and were the first to taste it.
It was delicious!

And as the newly married couple
rode away in their wedding coach
Rapunzel cried out happily …

"Best. Day. Ever!"

Snow White
and the
Great Jewel Hunt

By Kitty Richards
Illustrations by The Disney Storybook Artists

"Farewell, my love!" said Snow White. The Prince was leaving on a royal trip. It was the first time the newlyweds would be apart.

"I'll be home soon," replied the Prince. "Until then, I've left an envelope for you on the well. It's the first clue in a treasure hunt. At the end, you'll find a special gift!"

"Why, a well is where we first met," Snow White told the Seven Dwarfs.

The clue was in plain sight.
The Dwarfs gathered around as
Snow White opened the envelope.

"I wonder what the gift will be?" she said, then she read:

"Can't leave you a kiss,
Or even a hug,
So here is a clue:
Look under the...."

"I know!" cried Sneezy. "The Prince left the next clue under a bug!"

Sleepy yawned. "Bug?" he asked.

"Are you sure?" said Snow White.

Sneezy nodded and led everyone to the garden.

Snow White and the Dwarfs looked under ladybirds, butterflies, beetles and, very carefully, bumblebees. But they didn't find a thing.

"Actually, it would be pretty hard to hide a clue under a bug," said Snow White. "Maybe it's hidden under something that sounds like bug?"

"Under a jug?" suggested Happy.

"No, he must have meant under a mug!" said Grumpy.

Back inside, Grumpy announced, "To the kitchen!"
Then he nearly tripped over Dopey.

"Crawling on the floor in someone's castle is mad banners,"
scolded Doc. "I mean, it's bad manners!"

"Whatever are you doing, Dopey?" asked Snow White.

Dopey crawled out from under the carpet and held up an envelope. Snow White clapped her hands with excitement. "Under the rug! Oh, Dopey, you're a genius!"

Snow White read the clue:

"Hooray, you found it!
Easy when you try.
Now in the kitchen
Just lift up the...."

"Pie!" shouted all the Dwarfs at the same time.
Searching had given them quite an appetite!

First, Snow White served everyone a big piece of freshly baked fruit pie. Then, while they were eating, she read the next clue. It was hidden underneath the pie plate.

"Put on a smile,
It's no time to frown.
You'll find the next clue
In your royal...."

Snow White thought for a moment. "My royal gown?" she guessed.

In Snow White's dressing room, the Dwarfs searched through gown, after gown, after gown. But there was no clue to be found.

Ah-choo! "Now we'll never find Snow White's gift," said Sneezy.

Grumpy noticed Bashful standing in
the corner. "Why aren't you searching?"
Grumpy asked him.

"Why, he doesn't have to,"
Snow White said. "He's wearing my royal
crown. That must be where the clue is!"
Bashful took off the crown …

... and inside was the clue!

"The gift is almost yours.
My, my, this game has flown!
There's one thing left to do:
Just look upon your...."

"Stone!" offered Sneezy.
"That's silly," said Grumpy.
"It must be bone!"

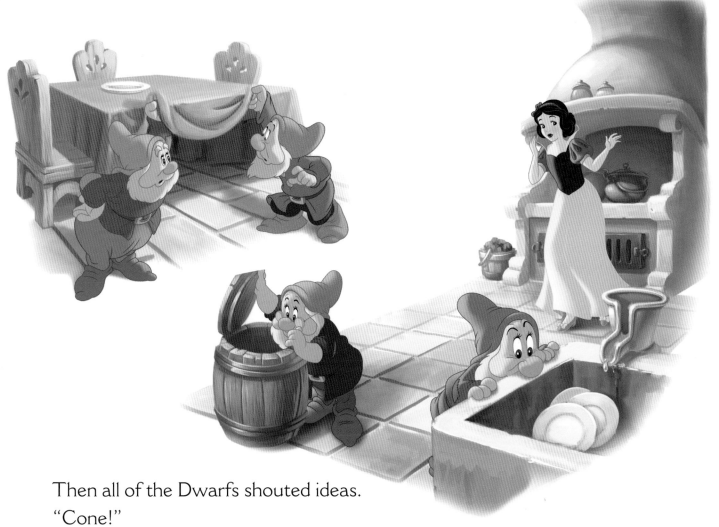

Then all of the Dwarfs shouted ideas.
"Cone!"
"Dome!"
"Trombone!"

As the Seven Dwarfs guessed,
Snow White realized someone was missing.
"Where's Sleepy?" she asked. They all set
off to look for him.

But he wasn't in the dining room.
Or in the kitchen.
Or in the Great Hall.

Sleepy was sound asleep on
Snow White's royal throne.

"That's the answer to the clue," she whispered.
"Just look upon your throne."
"So where's the gift?" Grumpy grumped.
"Right there," said Doc. "Look!"
Sitting at the very top of Snow White's throne
were two birds holding something that sparkled.
"This is so exciting!" said Happy.

To everyone's surprise, the birds flew down and placed a delicate necklace around Snow White's neck. The gift was a stunning heart-shaped ruby on a golden chain.

"Why, it's the colour of love," she said.

Doc saw that Snow White was holding something else. "The birds left a note!" he cried.

Snow White opened the envelope and read aloud:

"Yes, jewels are lovely,
But as this hunt ends,
Keep one thought in mind:
The best gifts are...."

"Odds and ends," said Sneezy.
"No, it's definitely chickens and hens," said Happy.

Grumpy couldn't believe his ears. "What's wrong with you fellas? The answer is friends!"

"You're right," said Snow White. "I love my new necklace, but the best part of today was the time we spent together. Friends are the greatest gift of all!"

Magical Activities

Complete these princess puzzles and activities,
then turn to page 100 for the answers.

"Magic Mirror on the wall, who is the fairest one of all?"
Draw yourself in the mirror.

Doc and Dopey are making a necklace for Snow White.
Can you colour it?

1 = RED   2 = YELLOW   3 = BLUE

Hi ho, hi ho. Who is off to work?
Cross out all the 'I's and 'T's to find out.

1. TDIOIPTEIY _____
2. IBTASITIHTFIUL _____
3. STINEETZIY _____
4. TSLIETEPTIY _____
5. IHTAIIPTPIY _____
6. IGRTIUMTPIY _____
7. TDIITOTIICT _____

Look at this picture of Snow White and her forest friends. Then answer the questions below.

1. How many birds? _____

2. How many butterflies? _____

3. How many rabbits? _____

4. How many squirrels? _____

5. How many turtles? _____

Help the Prince find the missing glass slipper. Circle the slipper that matches the one in the Prince's hand.

Draw a picture of yourself at the ball.

Prince Charming's Ball

Find the following words in the pumpkin carriage below.
(Hint: You will find the words going down and across.)

Cinderella
prince
slipper
Gus
midnight
mice
pumpkin
ball
stepmother
gown

a s t d p r s e m g
r m u d r i t s i n
t p r i n c e l d r
s p u m t r p i n s
g u s a s s m p i l
o m i c e r o p g a
w p b a l l t e h i
n k r s t m h r t e
c i n d e r e l l a
r n m p d u r p r w

Help Cinderella's friends finish the surprise! Colour the dress pink, the stars yellow and the hearts purple.

Can you match these sentences with the pictures they describe?
Write the number of each sentence in the
circle beside the correct picture.

3) Cinderella's friends help her get dressed.

2) The Fairy Godmother comforts Cinderella.

1) The shoe fits!

Help Prince Phillip save Princess Aurora.
Connect the dots to reveal his magic sword.

Help Prince Phillip find his way to the castle so he can awaken Princess Aurora with a kiss.

START

FINISH

What gifts do the fairies give to Princess Aurora when she is a baby? Use the code below to find out.

B	C	D	E	F	G	H	I	J	K	L	M	N	O	P	Q	R	S	T	U	V	W	X	Y	Z
2	3	4	5	6	7	8	9	10	11	12	13	14	15	16	17	18	19	20	21	22	23	24	25	26

Flora gives the gift of _____ .

2	5	1	21	20	25

Fauna gives the gift of _____ .

19	15	14	7

61

Number these pictures in the order they happened.

Connect the dots to see Briar Rose's dance partner.

There's magic happening! Can you find 7 things
that are different in the second picture?

Look at this picture of Ariel, Eric and their animal friends.
Then answer the questions below.

1. How many seagulls? _____   3. How many fish? _____

2. How many frogs? _____   4. How many flamingos? _____

Join Ariel as she explores the shipwreck!
Look for the names listed on the right in the puzzle below.
(Hint: You will find them going down and across.)

Prince Eric
Ariel
Flounder
King Triton
Max
Scuttle
Sebastian
Ursula

```
k r s e a d t c g m p
i e p a z u l l r a r
n o u r s u l a r f i
g d n i u o s s y l n
t e r e p a c r w o c
r l a l d n u o d u e
i s e b a s t i a n e
t d p r e g t s e d r
o r m a x p l t n e i
n i n c s s e d w r c
```

Eric and Ariel are collecting shells, stones and sticks on the beach. They've arranged them in two different patterns.

Can you finish each pattern by filling in the blank spaces with shells, stones or sticks?

1. _____ _____ _____

2. _____ _____

Everyone in the kitchen wants to cheer Belle up with a show.
Find the matching dishes, cups, forks and knives.
Circle the ones that are the same.

There are 7 odd and silly things happening in this picture. Can you find them all? Here are some hints:

- What's Gaston wearing on his head?
- There's a fire somewhere.
- Someone is walking on his hands.
- What an odd-looking bicycle.

- Take a look at Gaston's feet.
- It looks like Belle is going swimming!
- An animal has escaped from the farm!

Be a reader like Belle!
Cut along the dotted lines to create two bookmarks.

Let's read a story together!

Reading can take you to far-off places!

© Disney

© Disney

Help Belle and the Beast build a snowman with eyes, arms, a nose and a mouth. Don't forget his hat and scarf!

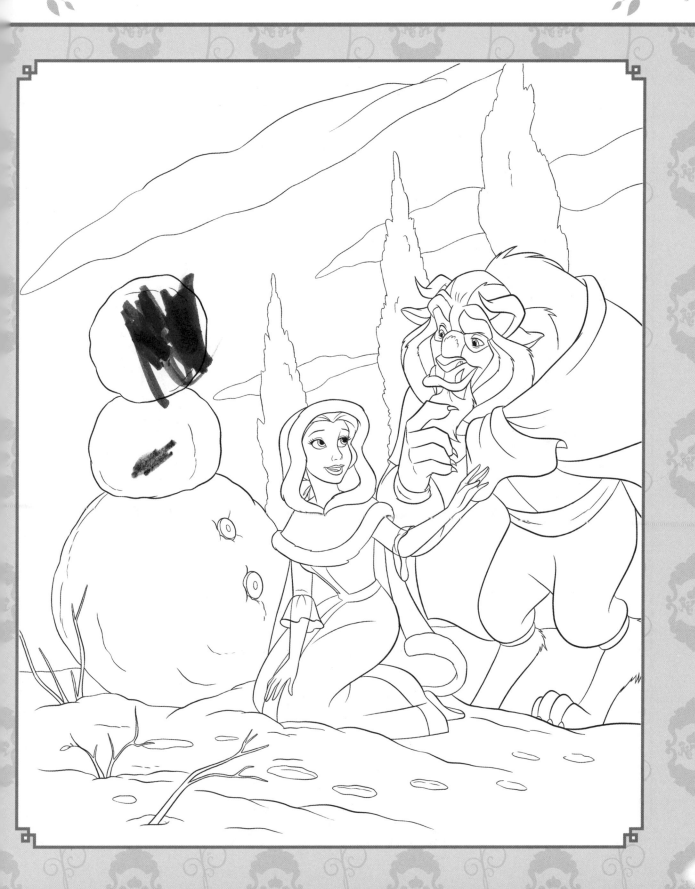

The Beast's Magic Mirror lets you see anyone you want.
Draw the person you would like to see in the Magic Mirror.

Write the names of the objects below in the crossword puzzle.

Across

1 4 6 7 8

Down

2 3 4 5

Can you find the following 10 objects hidden in the picture below?

- A glove
- A beach ball
- A cockerel
- A handbag
- A brush
- A cake
- A broom
- A pair of boots
- A comb
- A car

What kind of pet do Jasmine and Aladdin have?
Cross out all the 'u's and 'b's to find the answer to the riddle.

bau ufublubuyiunbg bucuabur-bupubuetb!

Use crayons or colouring pencils to colour
the palace and the city of Agrabah.

Jasmine and Aladdin are ready for a reading adventure!
Cut along the dotted lines to create two bookmarks.

Read a book
and discover
a whole new
world!

Every book
holds a new
adventure!

Jasmine wore the same outfit and accessories twice this week.
Which two days did she wear the same things?
_____ and _____

Look at this picture of Pocahontas, John Smith and their woodland friends. Then answer the questions below.

1. How many deer? _____   3. How many rabbits? _____

2. How many squirrels? _____   4. How many raccoons? _____

Help Pocahontas find her way through the forest to John Smith.

FINISH

START

How many butterflies do you see in the picture?
Write the number below.

I see _____ butterflies.

Meeko is hidden four times in the picture below.
Can you find him?

Complete this scene using the small pictures below.
Write the letter of each picture in the correct white box.

A   B   C   D

One of the canoes below matches Pocahontas's canoe.
Which one is it?

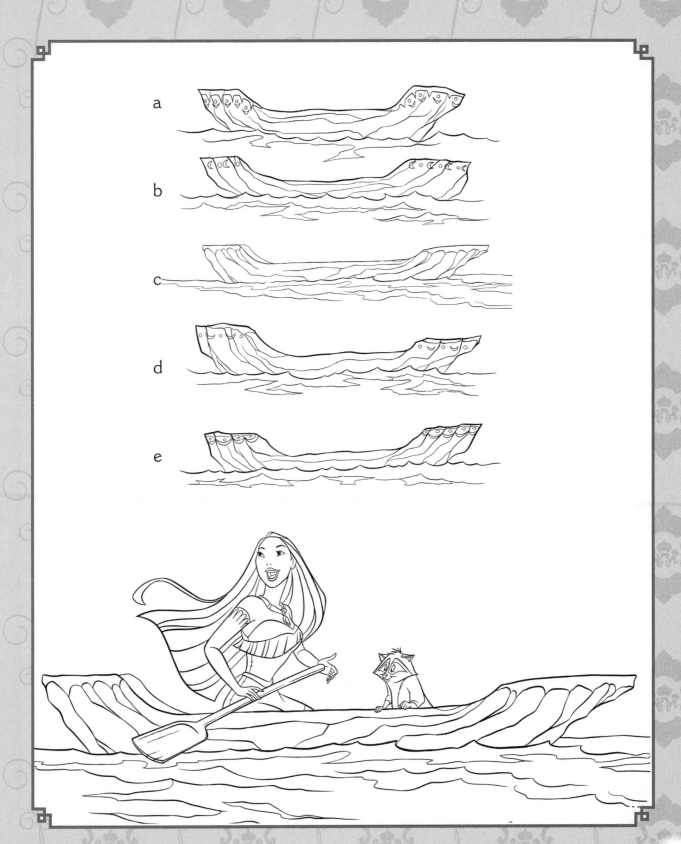

Write the names of the animals and objects below in the crossword puzzle.

Across

2

5

6

Down

1

3

4

Mulan needs to get to the Emperor. Can you help her?

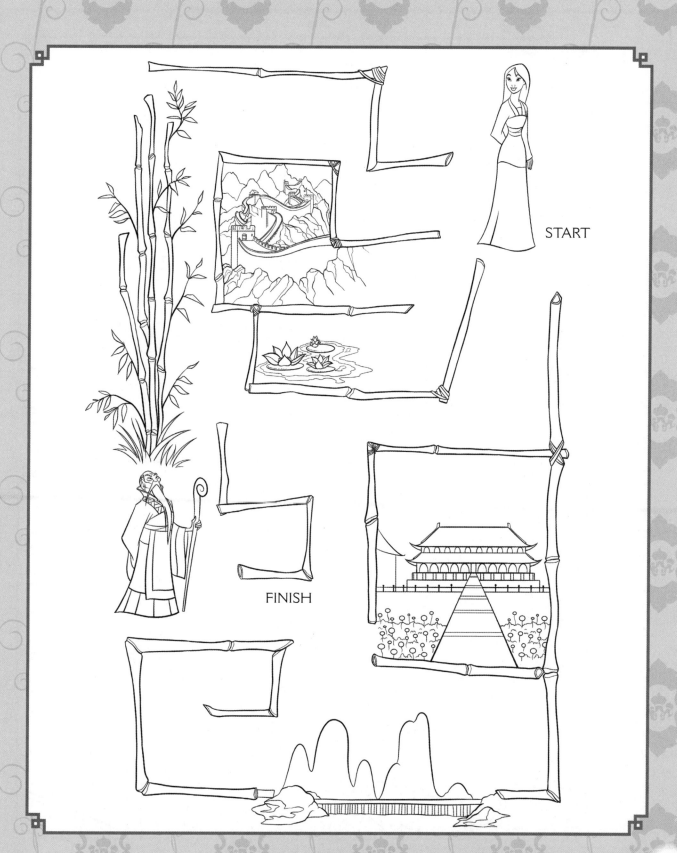

START

FINISH

Help Shang train his men. Can you find
six things that are different in the second picture?

Complete this scene with the small pictures below.
Write the letter of each picture in the correct white box.

A   B   C

Help the Matchmaker find the two Mulans who are the same.

1

2

3

4

5

6

7

8

9

Write the names of the people and things below in the crossword puzzle.

Across

3 5 7

Down

1 2 4 6

Each of the rows below must have four princesses:
Snow White, Aurora, Cinderella and Belle.
Fill each empty box with the correct letter.

A   B   C   D

Ask an adult help you cut out each picture, punch a hole at the top and thread a ribbon through the hole. Then decorate your room with these beautiful princesses!

Draw a picture of yourself as a princess on the back of the decorations.

© Disney

© Disney

© Disney

© Disney

sk an adult to help you cut out each picture, punch a hole at the top and thread a ribbon through the hole. Then decorate your room with these beautiful princesses!

Draw a picture of yourself as a princess on the back of the decorations.

© Disney

© Disney

© Disney

© Disney

Draw a line from each princess to her shadow.

Answers

Page 52
1. Dopey, 2. Bashful,
3. Sneezy, 4. Sleepy,
5. Happy, 6. Grumpy,
7. Doc.

Page 53
1. 4 birds, 2. 4 butterflies,
3. 3 rabbits, 4. 2 squirrels,
5. 1 turtle.

Page 54

Page 56

Page 58

Page 60

Page 61
Flora gives the gift of BEAUTY.
Fauna gives the gift of SONG.

Page 62

Page 64

Page 66
1. 2 seagulls, 2. 3 frogs,
3. 3 fish, 4. 3 flamingos.

Page 67

Page 68

Page 69

Page 70

Page 75

Page 76

Page 77
A flying car-pet.

Page 81
Tuesday and Thursday.

Page 82
1. 3 deer, 2. 4 squirrels,
3. 2 rabbits, 4. 1 raccoon.

Page 83

Page 84
I see 22 butterflies

Page 85

Page 86

Page 87
C matches Pocahontas's canoe.

Page 88

Page 89

Page 90

Page 91

Page 92
7 and 9

Page 93

Page 94

Page 99

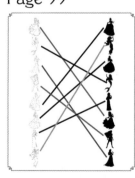

Beautiful Colouring

Use your favourite colouring pens or crayons to
make these princess pictures look magical.

Rapunzel does lots of chores in the tower.

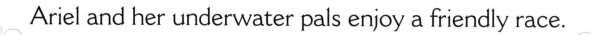

Ariel and her underwater pals enjoy a friendly race.

Ariel loves being a princess in a castle.

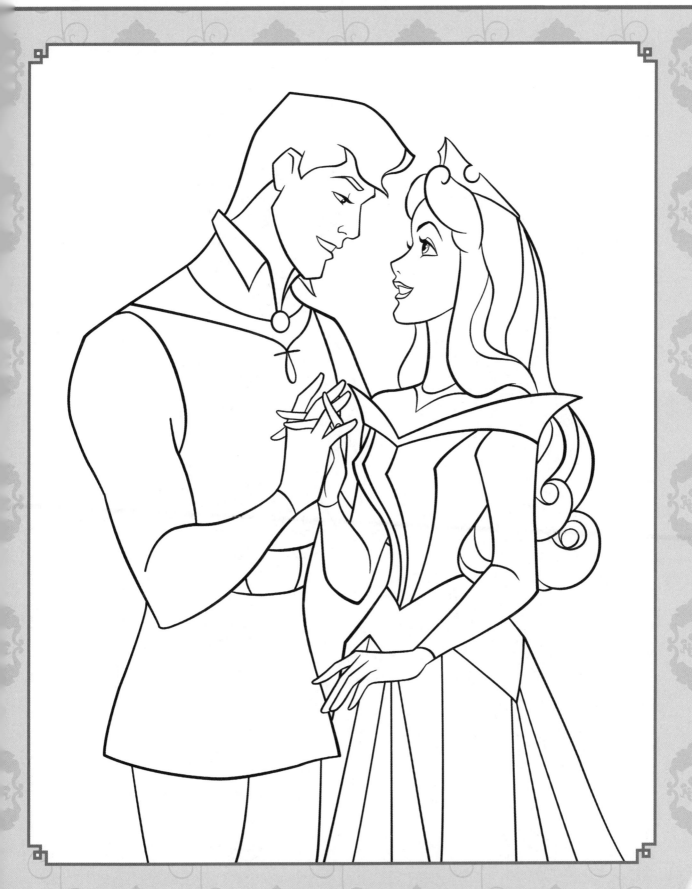

Tiana works hard to achieve her dreams.

Belle reads to the children of the village.

Belle likes to ride with Phillipe through the woods.

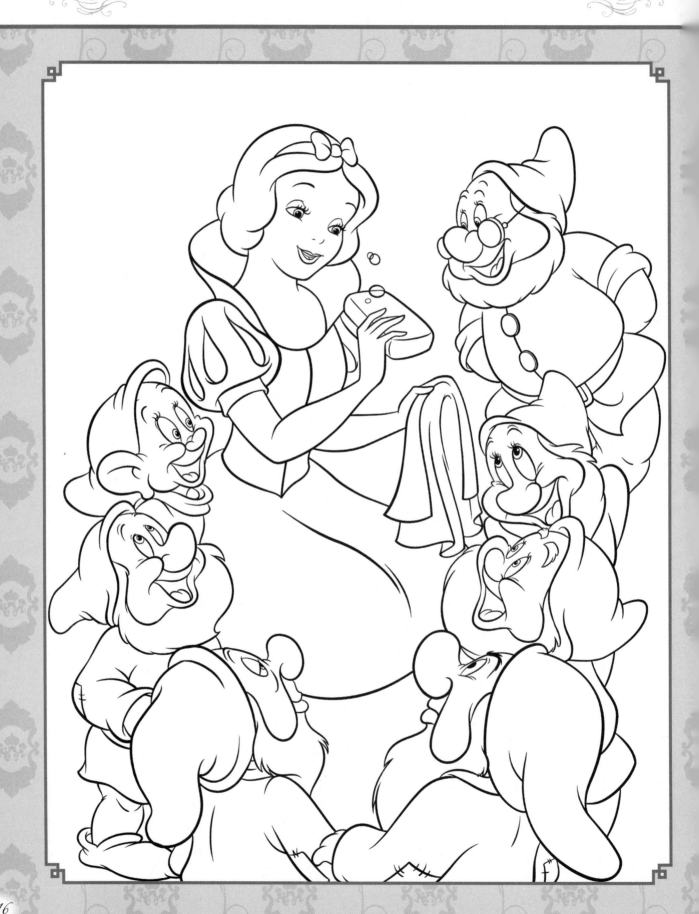

Merida hates it when her mum, Queen Elinor, brushes her hair.

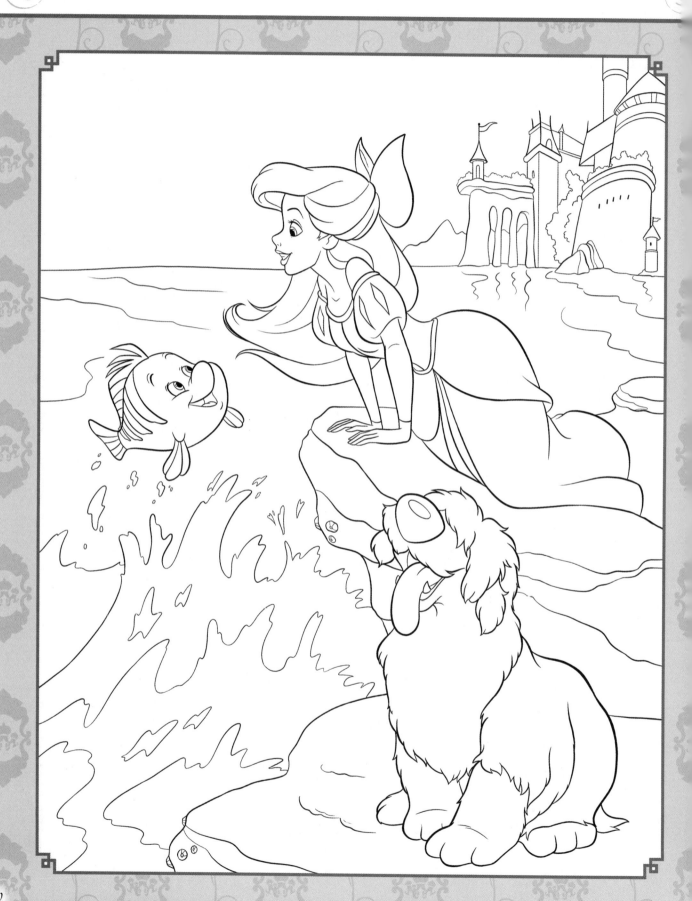

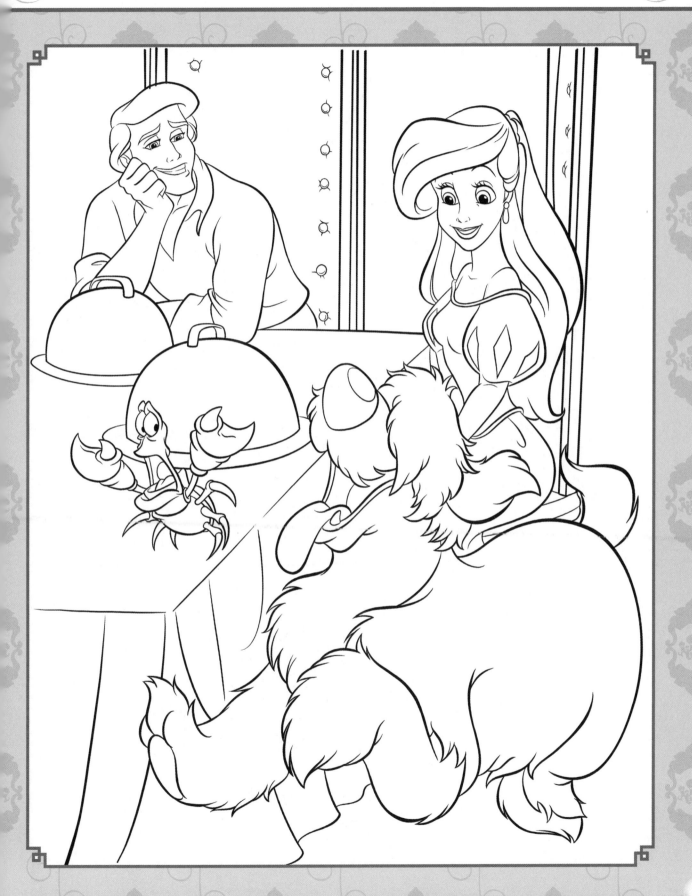

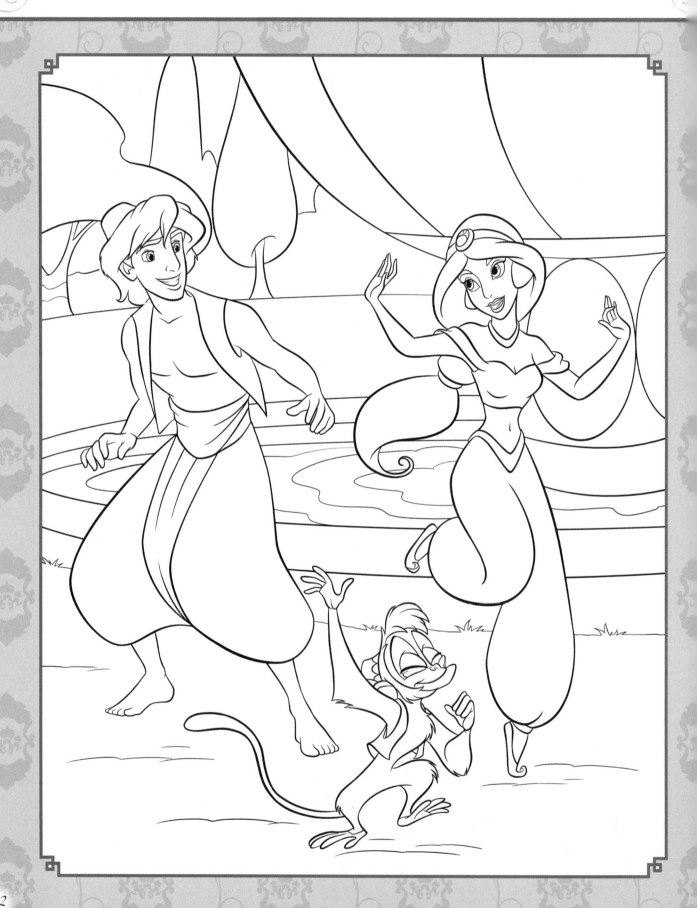

Jasmine and Aladdin try to count all the stars.

Aurora adds small sugar roses to a birthday cake.

Tiana looks like a princess.

Belle loves her father very much.

The Prince and Belle read their favourite book together.

Cinderella has made a special treat for Jaq's birthday.

Cinderella has decided what kind of pie to make.

Snow White and the Prince take a walk
in the meadow under the moonlight.

Rapunzel can't believe her eyes as she looks
in the window of the bookshop.

Rapunzel and Flynn share a quiet moment
on the lake as they wait for the floating lights.

Merida can't move in her formal dress!

"I'll be shooting for my own hand!"

The Genie always makes Jasmine's day.

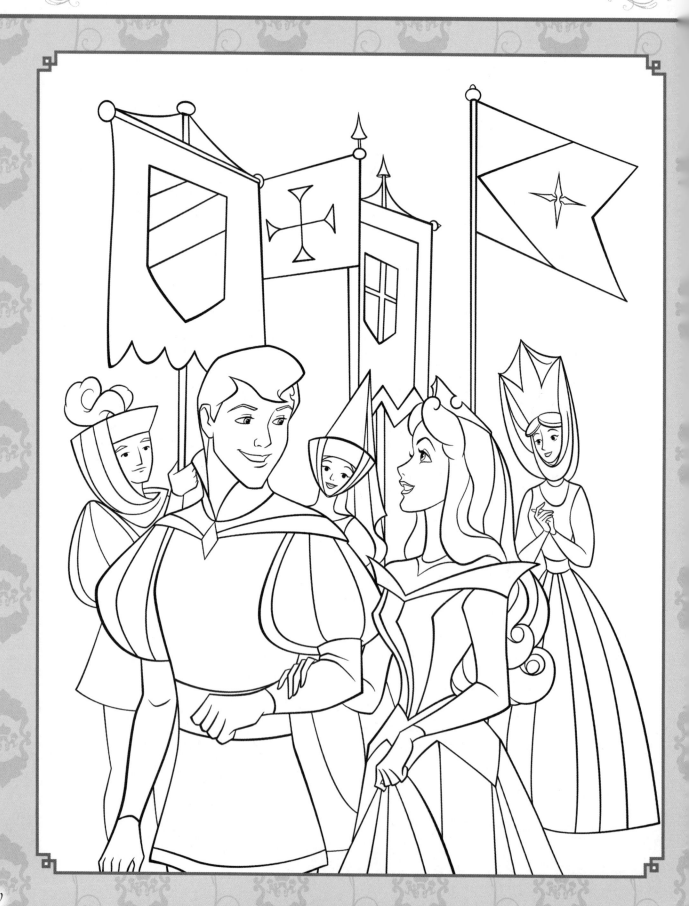

Belle's love broke the spell on the Beast and turned him back into a handsome prince.

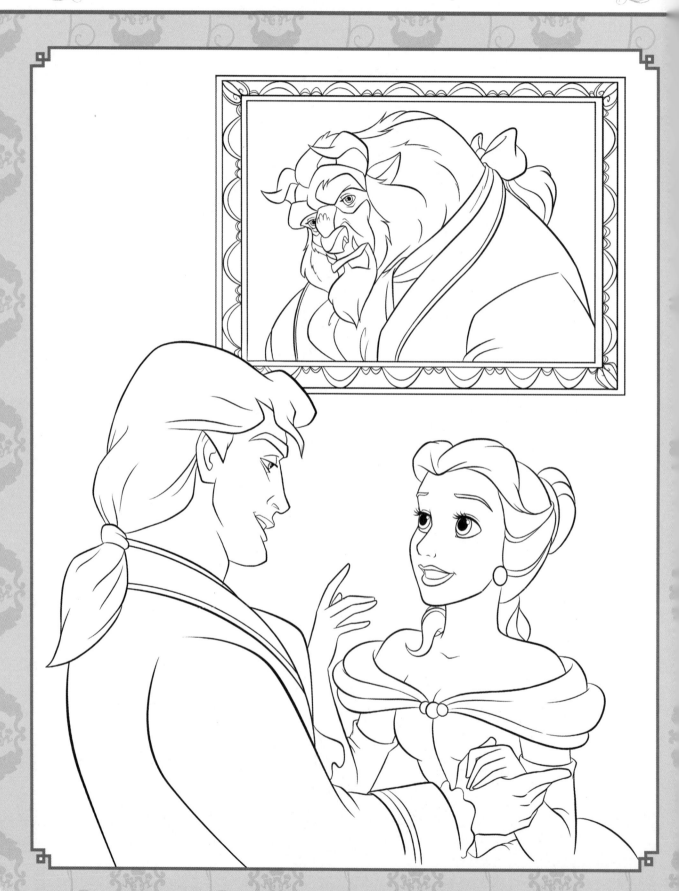

There are lots of things to buy at the market.

With help from her animal friends,
Cinderella sews a new suit for Prince Charming.

Cinderella's favourite vegetables
are broccoli and tomatoes.

Snow White feeds her bird friends.

Rapunzel is filled with wonder as she looks
at the floating lights up close for the very first time.

Flynn and Rapunzel launch their own lantern into the sky.

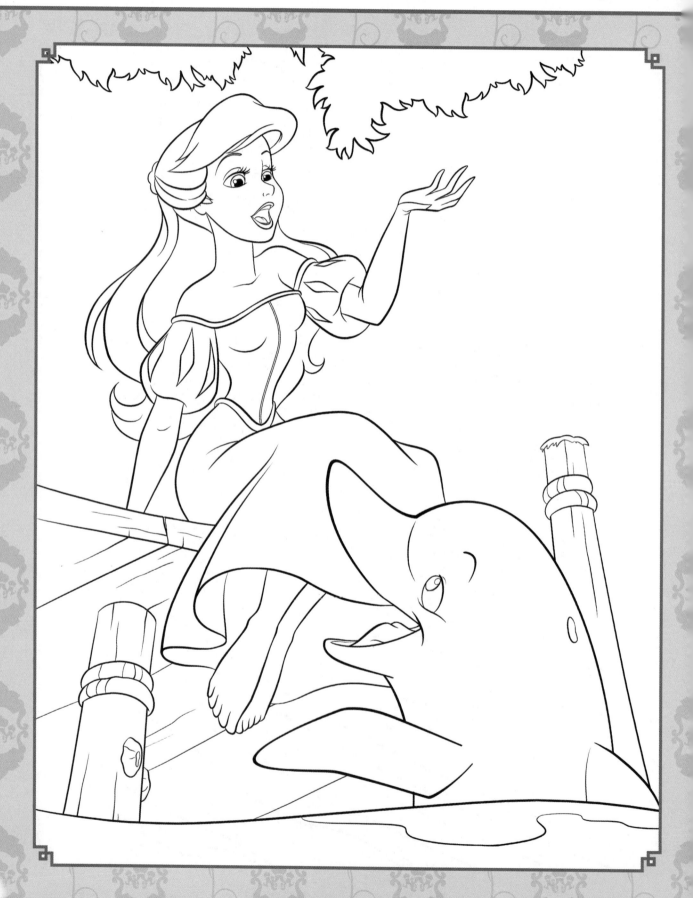

Merida's favourite thing to do is ride with
Angus through the forest.

Prince Phillip and Aurora go for
a ride through the countryside.

Aurora needs help deciding which tiara to wear today.

Tiana looks beautiful in the bayou!

Cinderella remembers the ball
and how she lost one slipper.

Cinderella gives Major a treat.

Merida is teaching Elinor-bear to fish.

Merida and the bear cubs are racing to save their mum!

As a reformed thief, Flynn sheepishly returns
the crown to its rightful owner.

Aurora loves listening to music.

Prince Charming and Cinderella
take Bruno for a brisk walk.

The Fairy Godmother joins
Cinderella for tea and a chat.

The Dwarfs give Snow White
a beautiful sparkling diamond.

Aurora
and the
Helpful Dragon

By Barbara Bazaldua
Illustrated by Studio IBOIX and Gabriella Matta

"I'll race you to the lookout point!" Princess Aurora called to Prince Phillip as they galloped through the forest one sunny autumn morning. She sped away on her horse, Moonlight, with Prince Phillip close behind.

Just as Aurora and Phillip rounded a bend, they heard a funny noise. A small dragon popped out from behind a tree and scampered towards Aurora.

"Oh, he's so cute!" Aurora exclaimed as she dismounted.

"Grrgrrgrr?" the little dragon murmured, clambering into Aurora's lap.

But Phillip wanted to protect his wife. "Dragons can be dangerous!" The little dragon shook his head.

"I think he's saying he's not dangerous," Aurora laughed. "Please, le take him home. I'm going to name him Crackle!"

"He does seem like a harmless little fellow," Phillip agreed.

But Moonlight was afraid. She tossed her mane and pawed the ground. Crackle's tail drooped sadly. Then he grinned a funny little grin. Suddenly, he licked Moonlight's nose with his long, warm tongue. Moonlight blinked with surprise and nuzzled Crackle under the chin. The little dragon giggled. "Moonlight likes Crackle!" Aurora laughed.

When Phillip and Aurora rode into the courtyard, the three
fairies were hanging banners for King Stefan and the Queen who
were coming for a ball that night.

"Come, my dear, let's practise dancing!" Phillip said to his princess.

But Flora gasped when she saw Crackle. "Dragons can
be dangerous."

"Remember the last one!" Fauna added.

"Oooh, I think he's sweet," Merryweather spoke up.

"Grrrgrr," Crackle babbled.

"He thinks you're sweet, too," Aurora told Merryweather as Prince
Phillip swept his princess across the courtyard.

Just then, Crackle noticed a kitten in Fauna's workbasket.

Crackle listened to the cute kitten purring. Crackle scrunched up his mouth and closed his eyes.

"Purrgrr, purrgrr!" Crackle tried to purr. Clouds of smoke puffed from his nose and mouth.

"Aachoo! Aachooooie! Ah-ah-ah-CHOO!" The fairies sneezed so hard that they fluttered backwards.

"Please – Achoo – stop trying to purr!" Fauna exclaimed.

Crackle looked sad for a moment. Then he saw the kitten playing with a ball of wool from the workbasket, and his eyes lit up. He snatched a ball of wool with his mouth. Whoosh! – it caught fire. Merryweather put the fire out with her wand.

"Oh, Crackle," Aurora said gently. "You're not a kitten. You're a dragon."

Crackle's lower lip trembled.

Just then, Crackle saw Phillip leading the horses into the stables. A dog followed Phillip, barking and wagging its tail. Crackle wagged his tail and ran to the stables, too.

"Woofgrr, woofgrr," he tried to bark. Flames shot from his mouth and set some straw on fire. Phillip poured water on the burning straw.

"You're not a dog," he said kindly, shooing Crackle away.

When Aurora saw Crackle
creep away from the stable, she carried
him into the castle and cuddled him on a
window seat.

A bird was singing outside.
Crackle's ears perked up and his eyes
shone hopefully.

"LAAAlaagrr!" he bellowed.

King Hubert heard the racket and
rushed into the room. "Oh, my, my, my!
How did a dragon get in here?"
he blustered.

Frightened by the king, Crackle jumped from the window seat and ran into the garden. Aurora chased after him.

At last she found the little dragon sitting beside a waterfall that splashed down from one pool to another. Crackle was studying a fish swimming in the lowest pool.

Before Aurora could stop him, Crackle splashed into the water. The startled fish leaped into a higher pool.

"Crackle, you're not a fish!" Aurora exclaimed as she pulled Crackle from the pool. "You're not a kitten, or a dog, or a bird either. You're a dragon!"

Tears rolled down Crackle's face. "Grrgrrgrr," he sobbed.

Suddenly, Aurora understood. "Do you think no one will like you because you're a dragon?" she asked.

Crackle nodded and whimpered sadly.

"Crackle, you can't change being a dragon," Aurora said kindly. "But you don't have to be a dangerous dragon. You can be a brave, helpful dragon."

Crackle stopped crying. "Grrgrrgrrgrr?" he growled hopefully.

Before Aurora could answer, thunder boomed and wind blew black clouds over the sun. Aurora snatched up Crackle. She reached the castle doors just as the rain began to pour down.

Everyone was gathered in the grand hallway, watching the storm.

"I'm afraid King Stefan and the Queen might lose their way on the road above the cliffs," Prince Phillip said, his voice filled with concern. "I should ride out to help."

Aurora looked at Crackle. "Do you want to show everyone that you're a brave and helpful dragon?" she asked.

"GRRRgrrrgrr!" Crackle exclaimed enthusiastically.

"Fly to the top of the highest castle tower," Aurora explained. "Then blow the largest, brightest flames you can." Aurora watched as the little fellow soared upwards. "Come on, everyone!" the princess called. She ran to get a better view of the watchtower, with Phillip and the others following closely behind.

Everyone tried to see Crackle at the top of the tower, but the storm was too dark and strong.

Suddenly, they saw huge flames, and they were coming from little Crackle! Gold and red light flashed up into the sky above the watchtower.

Again and again, Crackle blew his flames until, at last, Phillip shouted. "I see King Stefan and the Queen! They're almost here!"

Everyone hurried to greet the visiting royals.

"The tower light saved us!" King Stefan exclaimed. "I need one like it!"

At that moment Crackle flew down happily to join in the fun.

"Well, there he is! Our new tower light," King Hubert said with a laugh.

"A dragon?" King Stefan asked. "But dragons are dangerous...."

"Not Crackle," Aurora interrupted. "He's a brave and helpful dragon!"

That night at the ball, Crackle lit the candles, warmed food and kept the fireplace blazing. King Hubert and the fairies were so pleased that they took turns scratching Crackle beneath his chin.

As Prince Phillip and Aurora danced, Crackle trotted beside them. Outside, it was cold and stormy. But inside, everyone was happy and warm – especially Crackle the helpful dragon.

The End

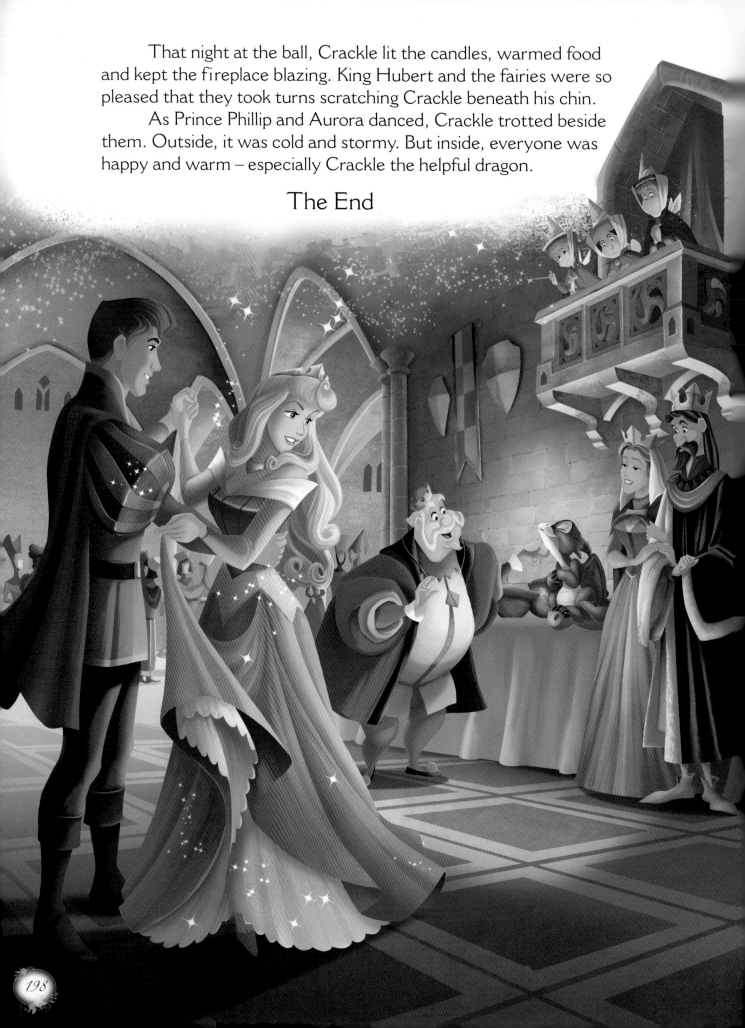

Ariel's Dolphin Adventure

By Lyra Spenser
Illustrated by IBOIX and Andrea Cagol

"Oh, Eric! This is wonderful!" Ariel said excitedly as she twirled around the ballroom with her prince. "I can dance with you and see the ocean!"

"Do you miss your sea friends?" he asked.

"Sometimes," Ariel replied a bit sadly. "But I love being with you."

Bright and early the next morning, Prince Eric found Ariel walking along the beach. He knew that she was hoping to see Flounder and Sebastian, as well as her other friends. Sadly, they were nowhere in sight.

202

Eric caught up with his princess and hugged her as they watched the white-capped waves crashing hard against the shoreline.

"It's rough out there today. If I were a fish, I think I might be too scared to come close to shore," Eric said gently. "Don't worry, Ariel. We'll figure out a way to bring together land and sea. You deserve the best of both worlds."

Later that day, Eric and Ariel
went for a walk.

"I was thinking about what you
said earlier," Ariel said. "I want to show you
something." She led him straight to a quiet,
beautiful little lagoon.

Eric grinned. "I almost kissed you for the
first time here."

"Eric, do you think my friends would feel
safer visiting me here?"

Eric rubbed his chin. "Hmmm. Maybe."

A few weeks later, Eric found Ariel walking along the beach again. "Come with me," he said. "I have a surprise for you."

He took her right to the lagoon. It now had a big wall to keep out dangerous sea creatures like sharks, but it also had a gate so that Ariel's friends could enter the lagoon. In fact, Flounder, Scuttle and Sebastian were there to greet her!

"Oh, Eric!" Ariel gasped. "I love it!"

Ariel was so excited that she waded into the water.
Then she stopped, seeing something else in the lagoon. "Look!"
she exclaimed. As they watched, a baby dolphin leaped out of the
water! "He's just a baby. I wonder where his mother is."

Flounder swam across the lagoon, but the baby dolphin raced away.

"Poor little guy," Flounder said. "He seems scared of me."

"We should find his mother right away!" Ariel said as she gently coaxed the baby to swim over to her.

"I bet she's on the other side of that wall. Don't worry, Ariel!" Flounder said. "We'll find her!"

But Sebastian and Flounder couldn't find the dolphin's mother. "Oh, Ariel! This is terrible," Sebastian said a few days later. "We have looked everywhere under the sea, but cannot find the baby's mother. King Triton will be so angry!"

Ariel was watching the little dolphin swim slowly around the lagoon. Heartbroken, she knew that the confused baby was looking for his mother.

Later that night Ariel awoke to the sound of a
loud clap of thunder. From the safety of the palace, she
saw terrible, high waves crashing to the shore.

"Ariel?" Eric asked. "Are you worried about that baby dolphin?"

"Oh, Eric, I am. He must be terrified," she shuddered in reply.
"We need to go to him. And, Eric? I need to ask my father for help."

Eric felt terrible. He now understood that he had made a bad decision by closing in the lagoon. He followed Ariel into the stormy night, ready to help in any way he could.

When they arrived at the lagoon, Flounder was trying to calm the frightened baby dolphin.

"Go to the baby dolphin, Eric,"
Ariel said gently. "He feels safe with you."
Ariel looked into her prince's eyes, letting him
know that she trusted him with her sea friends.

Ariel climbed carefully out onto the wall of the lagoon and called to all the sea creatures. "Help me, please!" she cried out. "I am Ariel, princess of the seas. I need my father, King Triton. Please help!" Below the surface, sea creatures raced to find King Triton.

215

Eric tried to keep the baby dolphin safe
from the crashing waves. Holding him, Eric led
him to calmer waters near some rocks.

Suddenly, there was a flash of light, and
the storm calmed.

King Triton had arrived at the lagoon.

"What has happened here?" King Triton roared.

Eric looked down humbly. "It is entirely my fault, Sir," he explained. "I built this wall to make a nice place for Ariel to visit her friends. I was wrong."

The king of the seas glared at Eric. Then with a hint of a smile, he added, "Well, you are human, after all."

With a wave of his trident, King Triton called to all the dolphins and they quickly found the baby dolphin's mother! Frantically, she tried to get into the lagoon.

"Oh, dear!" Ariel exclaimed. "The gate won't open! She can't get in!"

Eric looked at King Triton. "Do you mind...?"

"Not at all," the king replied. "Swim back, everyone!"

He raised his trident and blasted down the wall.

There was no royal ball that night at the palace. Instead, Eric and Ariel returned to the lagoon and danced under the sparkling stars.

"I love this place," Ariel said to her husband. "Thank you."

Just then the baby dolphin and his mother entered the lagoon, surfaced and playfully splashed the prince and princess.

"I think that means we are forgiven!" Ariel laughed.